DEDICATION

To

Robyn and John

This Book Belongs to

MOVING
to a NEW HOME

by
WANDA HAYES

illustrated by
FLORENCE MASTERS

STANDARD PUBLISHING
Cincinnati, Ohio   3039   Printed in U.S.A.

"We have a big surprise today.
Our moving day is one week away.
We'll live in a house high on a hill.
You're going to like it. We know you will."

We're going to move away someday.
I wonder—will I have a nice place to play?

This is my home where I play with my dog.
I can take a hike and catch a frog.

My house, the yard, and all about
Are places where I can sing and shout.

We're going to move away someday.
I wonder—will I have a nice place to play?

I'll be in a new neighborhood.

Good-bye, milkman and mailman and friends at the store.
I won't be stopping to talk anymore.

Good-bye to the park and my favorite tree.
When the boys and girls come, they won't see me.

I'll be in a new neighborhood.
I'll be in a new neighborhood.

What will my new room be like?

Will the pictures and windows and floor be the same?
Will I have a space for each book, toy, and game?

Will the walls be yellow or blue or red?
Can I still keep my football under my bed?

What will my new room be like?
What will my new room be like?

I love my old Sunday school.

A picture of Jesus smiles down from the wall.
I think that it is my favorite of all.

I sit at a table that's just my size
And find a new book—a pleasant surprise.

I like my old Sunday school,
My bright and pretty Sunday school.

I love my Sunday-school friends.

There are Kent and Carolyn, Cristine and Kerri,
Laura and Jimmy, Steven and Sherri.

We sit on a big rug and listen to teacher.
She sits down where we are so we can reach her.

I have lots of Sunday-school friends.
I love my Sunday-school friends.

I have fun with my Sunday-school friends.

Sometimes we sit down, and sometimes we stand.
We march and play music and make our own band.

We pray to God and sing songs about Jesus.
We try to please Him, and we know that He sees us.

Good-bye to you, Sunday-school friends.
I'll miss you, Sunday-school friends.

Today was our big moving day.

I packed my toys for the moving man
And watched him load them in the big van.

My friends came to watch,
 and they all waved good-bye.
"Come and see me," I said.
 But I wanted to cry.

Today was the busiest day.
Today was our big moving day.

Guess what I found
in my new neighborhood?

A milkman

and mailman
and a new grocery store.

The groceryman winked
when I walked in the door.

Right by my house there's a nice place to play,
And I met some new children the very first day.

I like what I found in my new neighborhood.
My mother was right. She said that I would.

Guess what I found in my brand new house?

A bright room with rugs and curtains of red.
There are all my old toys and my very own bed.

Mom and Dad fixed this room especially for me.
It's the prettiest room I ever did see.

That's what I found in my new house tonight.
Daddy said I'd like it. You know? He was right.

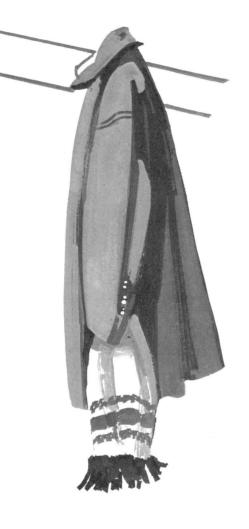

Guess what I found at
my new Sunday school?

There was a hook for my coat

and a chair just my size,

A smiling teacher
with twink-e-ly eyes.

Books on the table and pictures on the wall.
It's almost not like a new place at all.

The teacher told a story I knew.
I like this Sunday school. I really do.

Guess who I met at my new Sunday school?

I didn't see Carolyn, or Laura, or Jimmy.
But I made two new friends—Jeffrey and Kimmy.

We even sang my favorite song.
This kind of Sunday school is where I belong.

This is a good Sunday school.
Just like my old Sunday school.

Dear God in heaven,

My yard and room and everything new
Are wonderful gifts. Thank you. Thank you.

Thank you for all friends—each old and new one.
Wherever I am, they help me have fun.

I'm happy today because I know
That you will be with me wherever I go.

Thank you for my new home.

In Jesus' name. Amen.